WHAT'S INSIDE?

by Barbara Shook Hazen

illustrated by Richard Erdoes

THE LION PRESS

Publishers, New York

Published by The Lion Press, Inc.
21 West 38th Street, New York, N.Y. 10018.
Published simultaneously in Canada by George J. McLeod Ltd.
73 Bathurst Street, Toronto 2B, Ontario.
This book was printed and bound in Belgium.
Library of Congress Catalog Card Number: 68-9414

To Brack, Caesar the Cat — and Curiosity

Many things around us
have secrets that they hide.
Look and see if you can guess —
what's inside.

A hollow log.
Is anyone there?

Maybe a berry-eating bear?

Or a sly old weasel trying
to scare you away.

Not Today!

In his furry underwear,
A fat raccoon is peeling a pear!

Fern fronds curled
are a small green world,
and someone's there
on a blade-bent chair.
Let's look and see.
Who can it be?

A glowworm lighting up his tail?

A June bug with his acorn pail?

No! Follow along this glistening trail till you come upon a silver snail.

In the meadow as you pass,

who is hidden in the grass?

A caterpillar who's lost a shoe?

Or a rabbit playing peek-a-boo!

No!
Field mice in a grass-lined nest
tucked away for their afternoon rest.

Bright red rose
with your petals closed,
what do you hide
inside?

Is there a tiny elf
tucked upon your flower shelf?

Or could there be
a dancing flea
having a dainty sip of tea?

No! Curled up cozy, safe and snug
Is a sleeping lady bug.

Here's an egg of enormous size.
What could be its surprise?

A dragon with scales?
Twin newborn whales?

No!
A baby bird — pick-pick-pick.
Soon we will see an ostrich chick.

High in the vine-twined jungle trees
someone lives in a penthouse of leaves.

Who? A python in a squeeze?
Or a talking parrot who likes to tease?

No! A happy orangutan who prefers his tree house to the zoo.

Mud and sticks and reeds and weeds
make a house just right for the needs

Of a flounder afloat?
Or a goat in a boat?

No, no, no!
Neither is so.

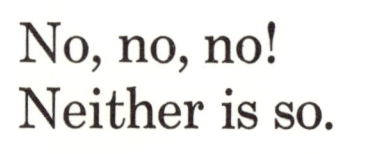

This house was built without one nail
by a beaver with a paddle-whack tail.

What's inside the hole in the tree?
A honey-hungry bumblebee?

A calico cat, an acrobat?
Or maybe the wicked robber rat
who ran away with the farmer's hat.

Inside is an owl
with green-gold eyes.
He's very old
and very wise —
for he always asks questions
and *never* tells lies.

Kangaroo, kangaroo,
stop your hopping, tell us, do,
what you carry in your pocket?

Could it be a long gold locket?
A box of buttons, beads, and bows?
Patent slippers and party clothes?

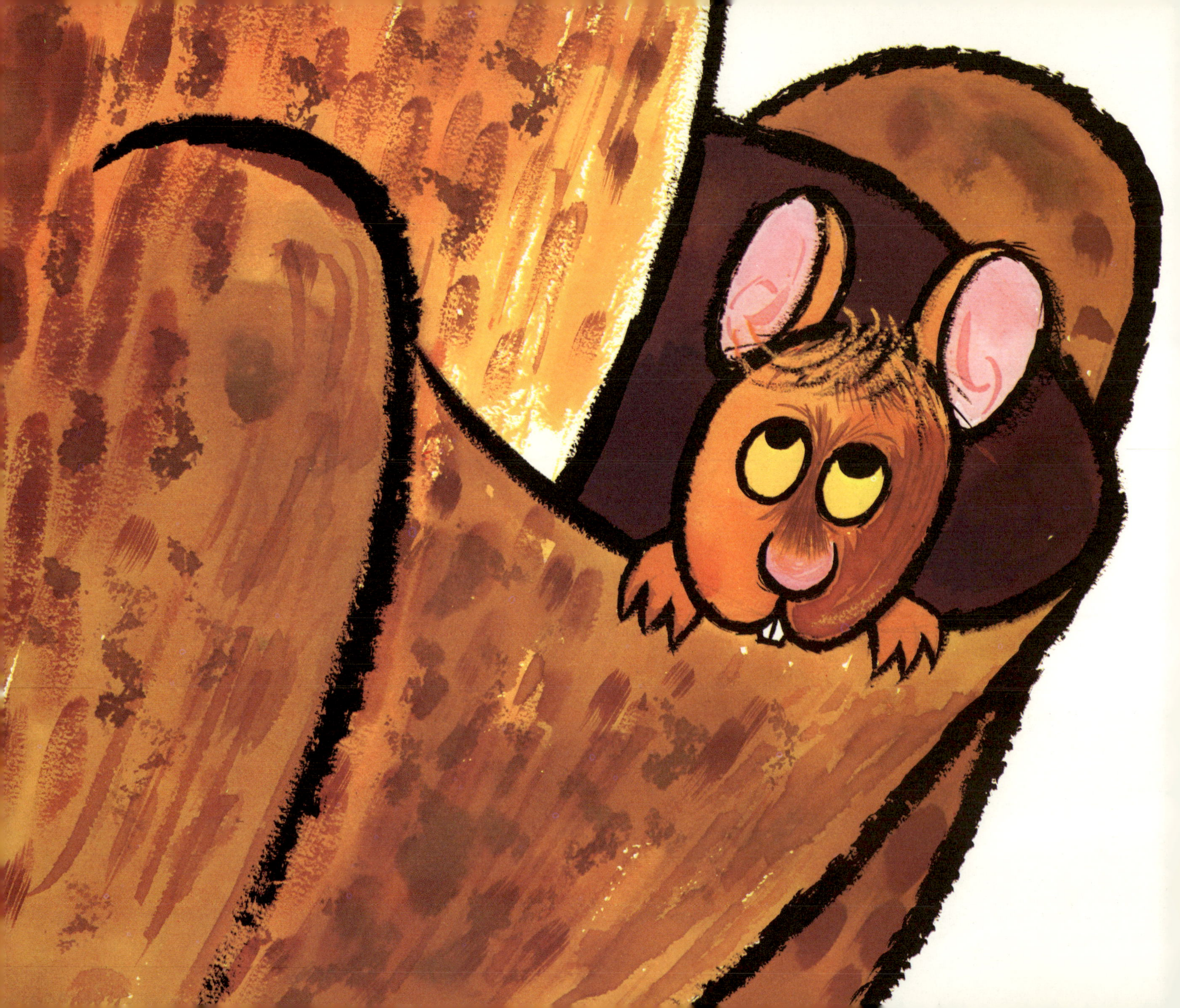

No, No! None of these —
not buttons, beads or party clothes,
I carry my son, my Joey, who
is a baby kangaroo.

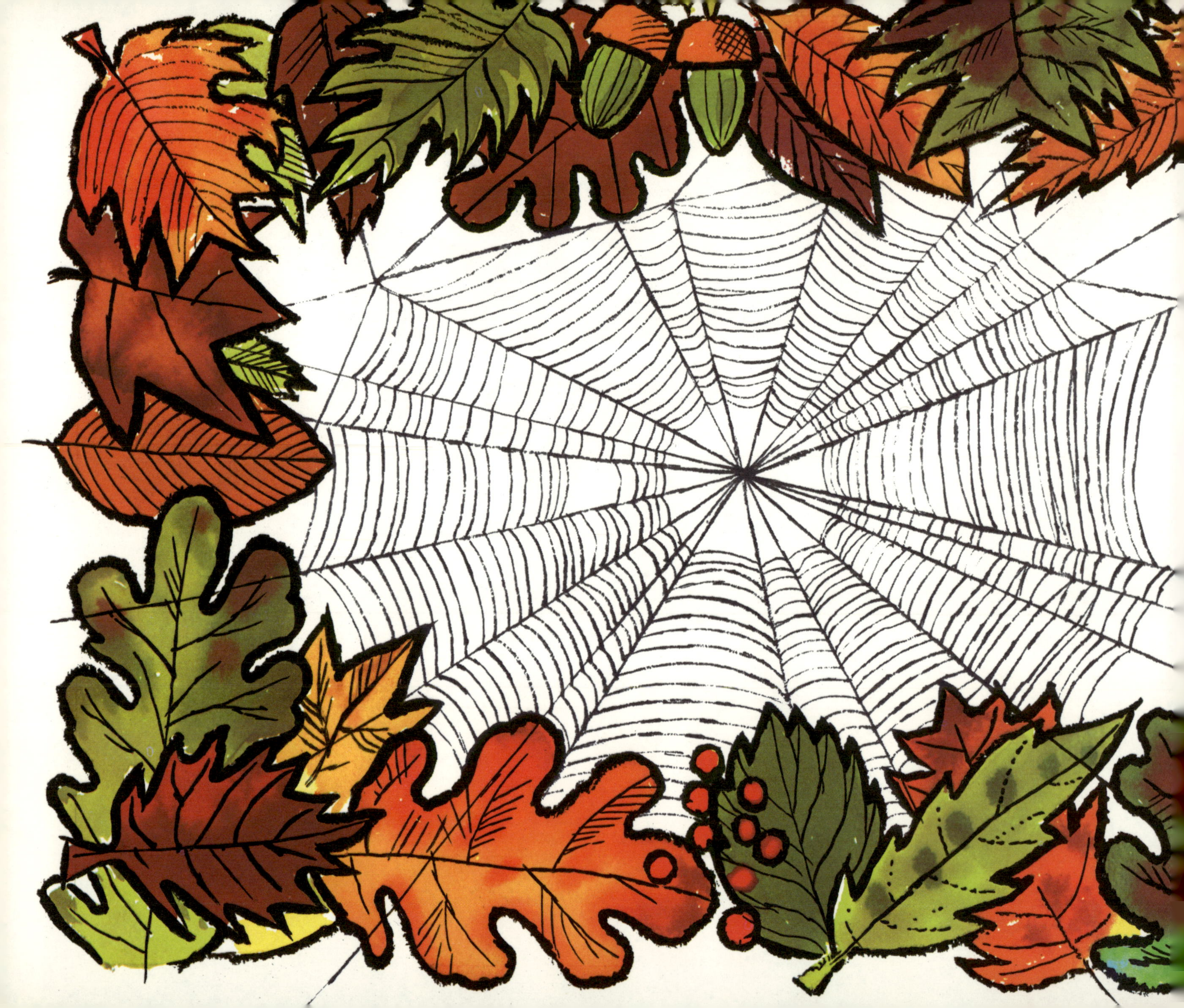

Is anyone small enough to get inside this lacy web of net?

A frightened fly?

Or a wasp who's shy?

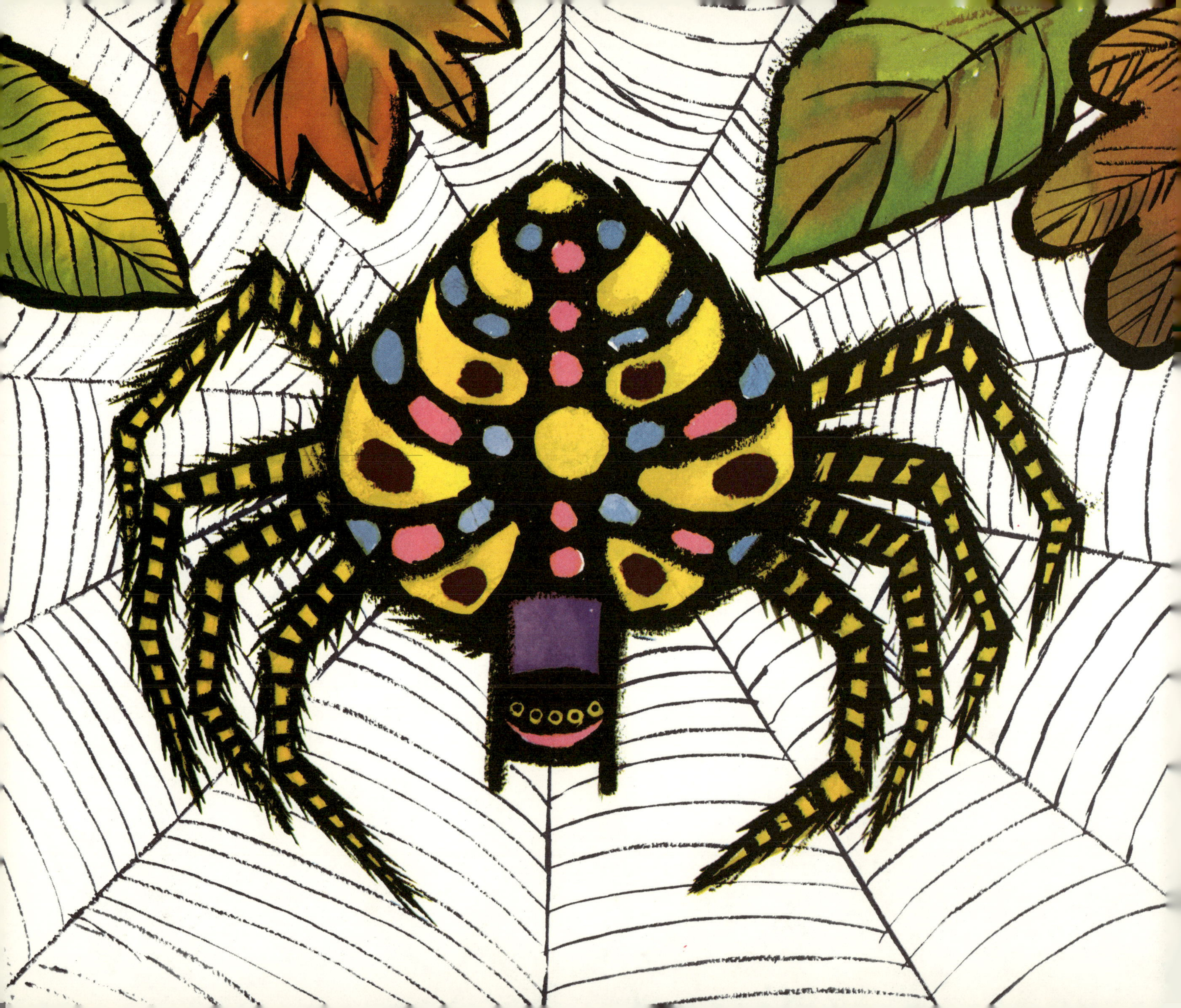

Me, says the spider.
I live alone.
I weave my own yarn
I spin my own home,
and of the finest
thread it's sewn.

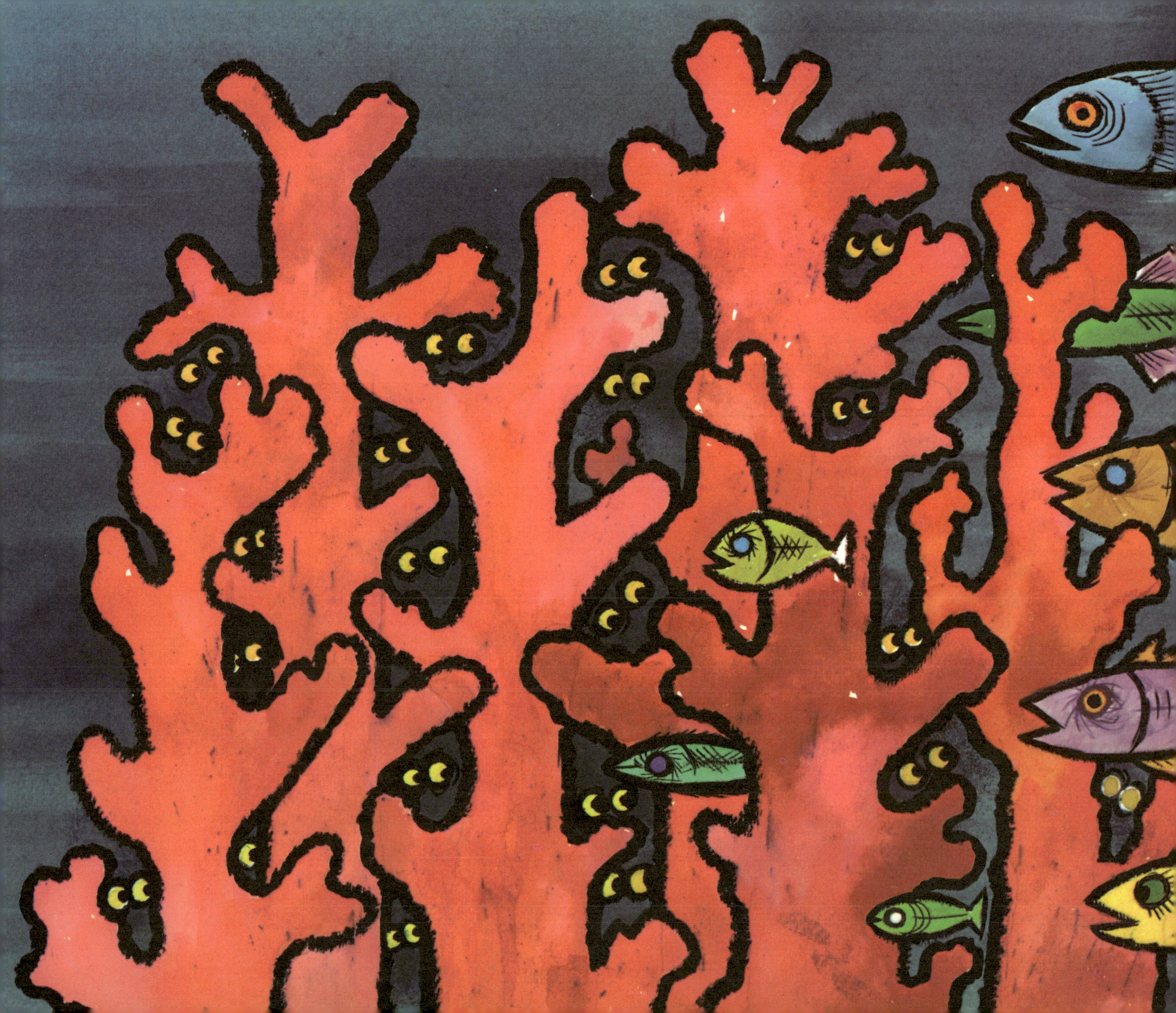

A coral castle
with shells in the halls
and seaweed curtains
on the walls.

Is someone at home and happy there?
Is it a mermaid combing her hair?
An octopus trying to climb the stair?
Is it an eel eating a meal?

Inside are seven oyster girls

playing jacks with pale pink pearls.

The pelican's beak is deep and wide.
And guess what he keeps inside?

A bunch of bananas?

Or bright red bandanas?

Games to play
on a rainy day?

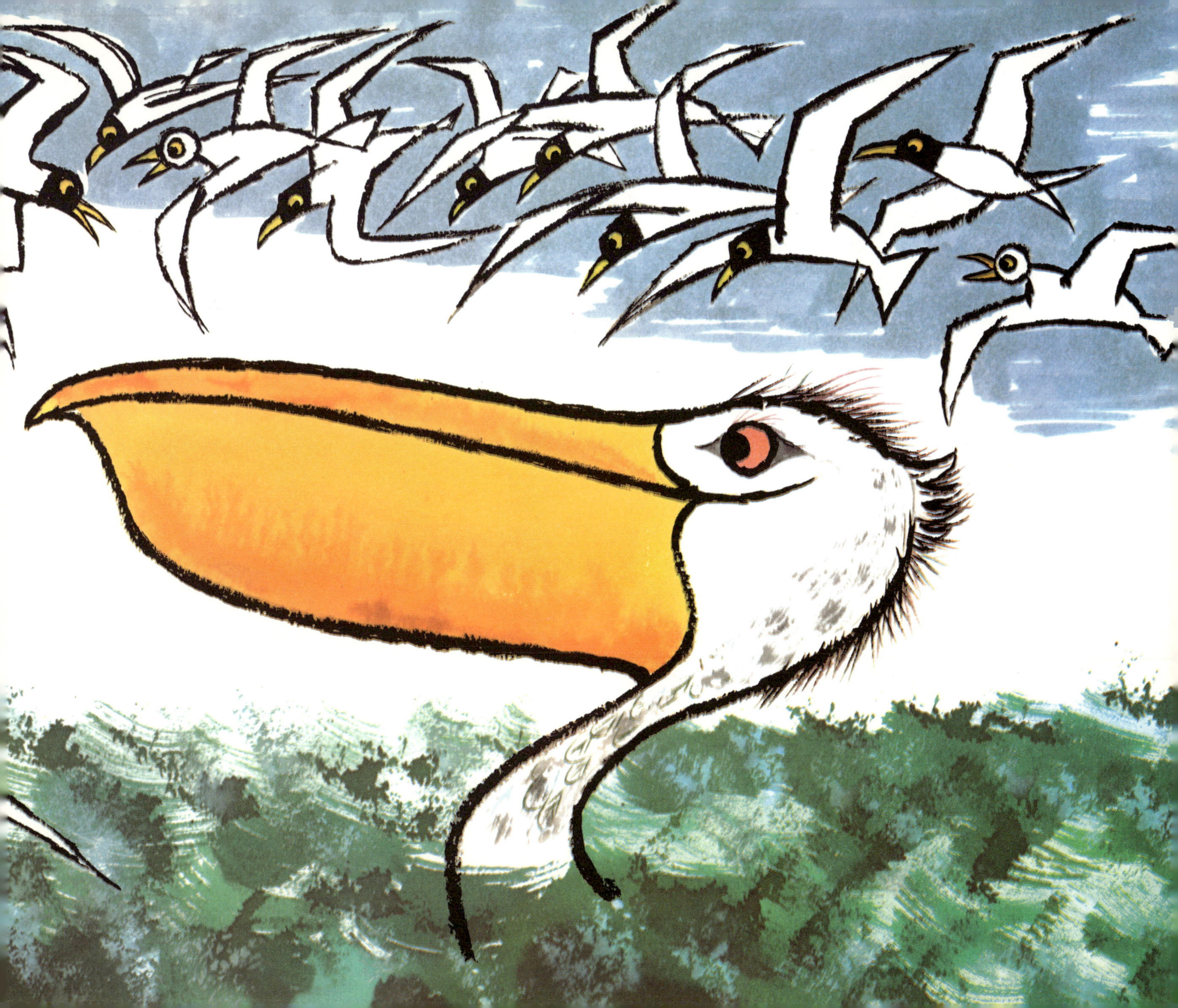

No! It's a fish — and he's getting away!

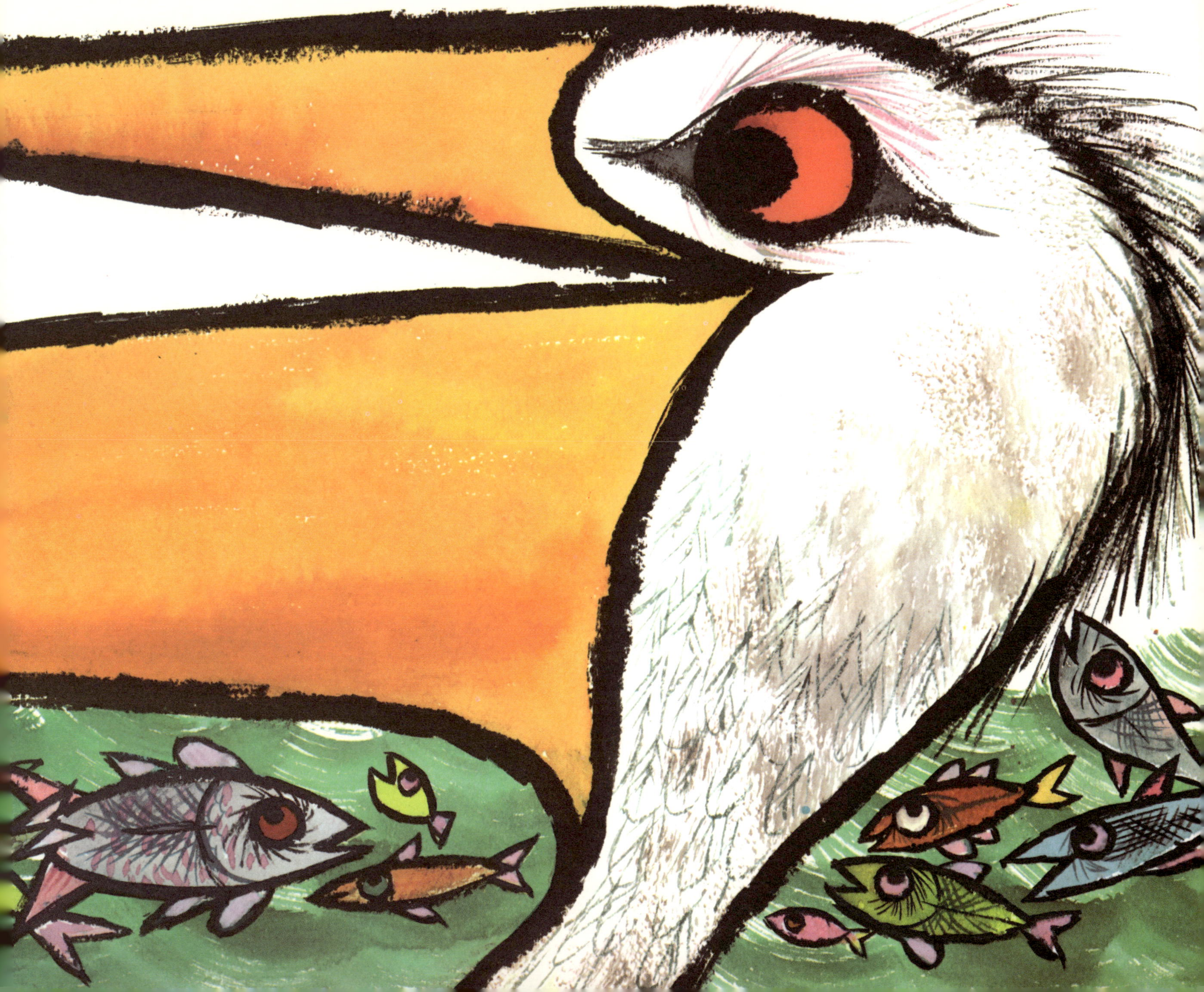

A mound of ground.
Let's look around
for just a minute
and see what's in it.

Buried gold?
Or a chipmunk bold?

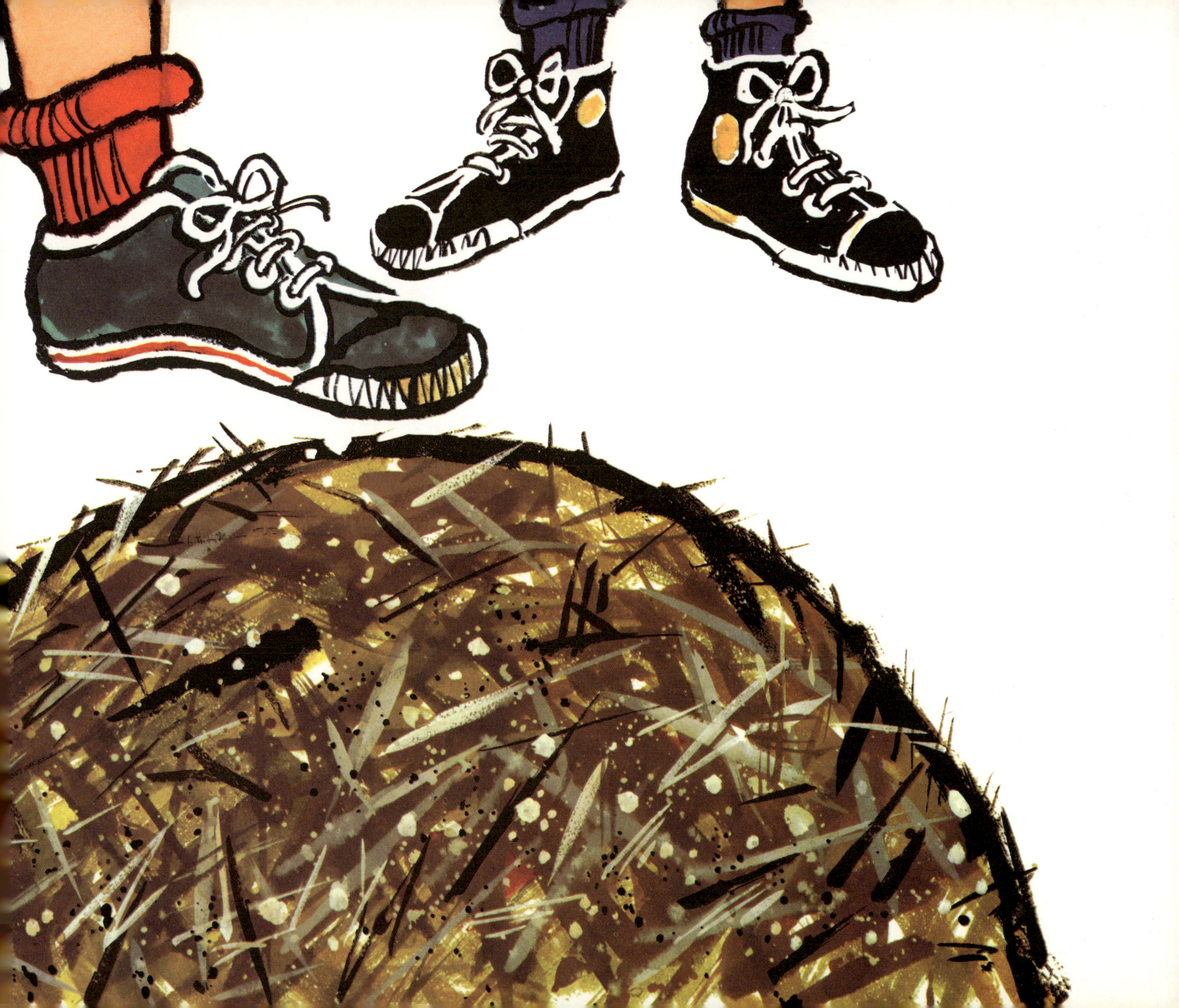

Ants! Ants by the dozens — aunts, uncles and cousins, ant fathers and mothers, ant sisters and brothers are housed in the ground inside this mound.

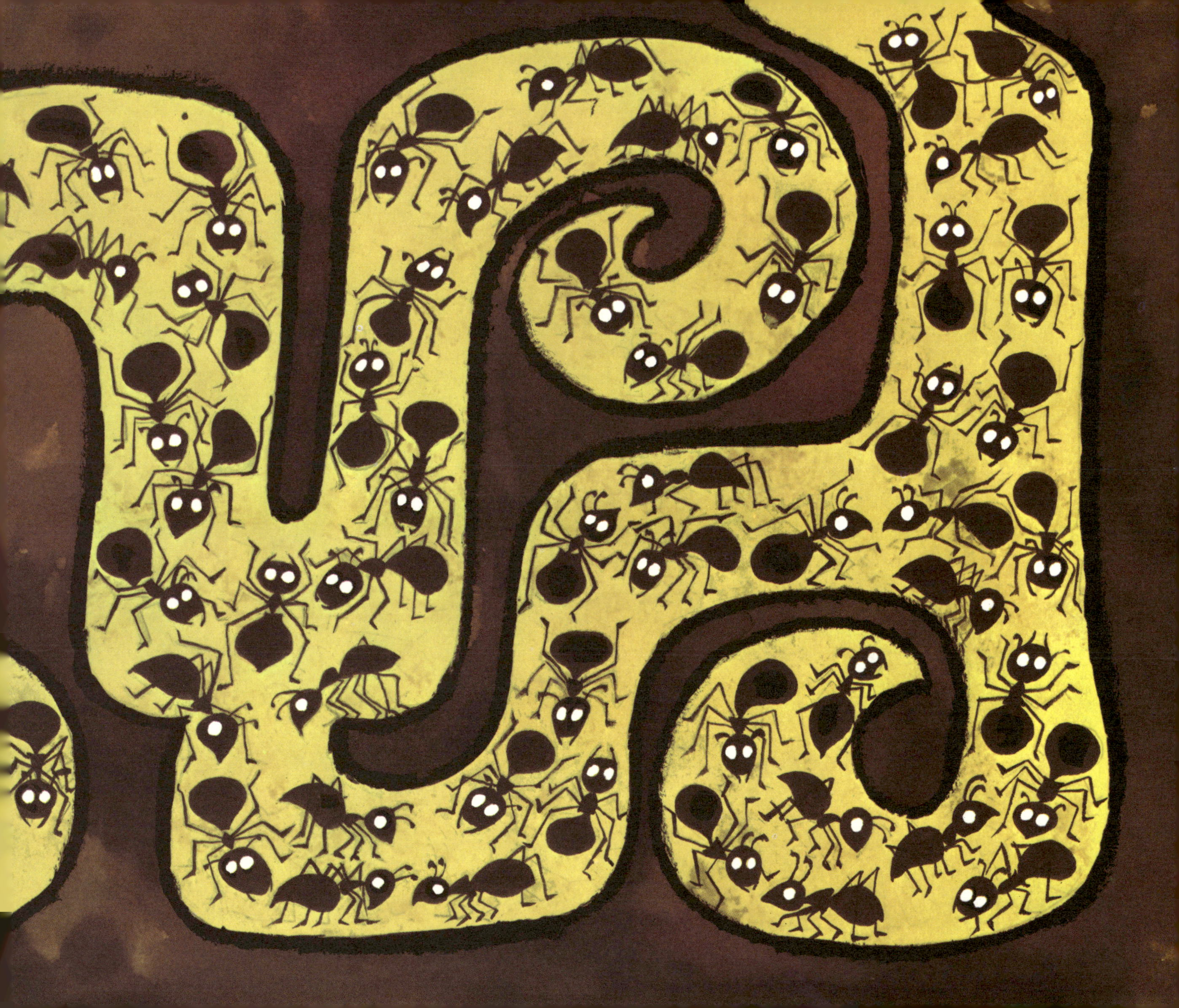

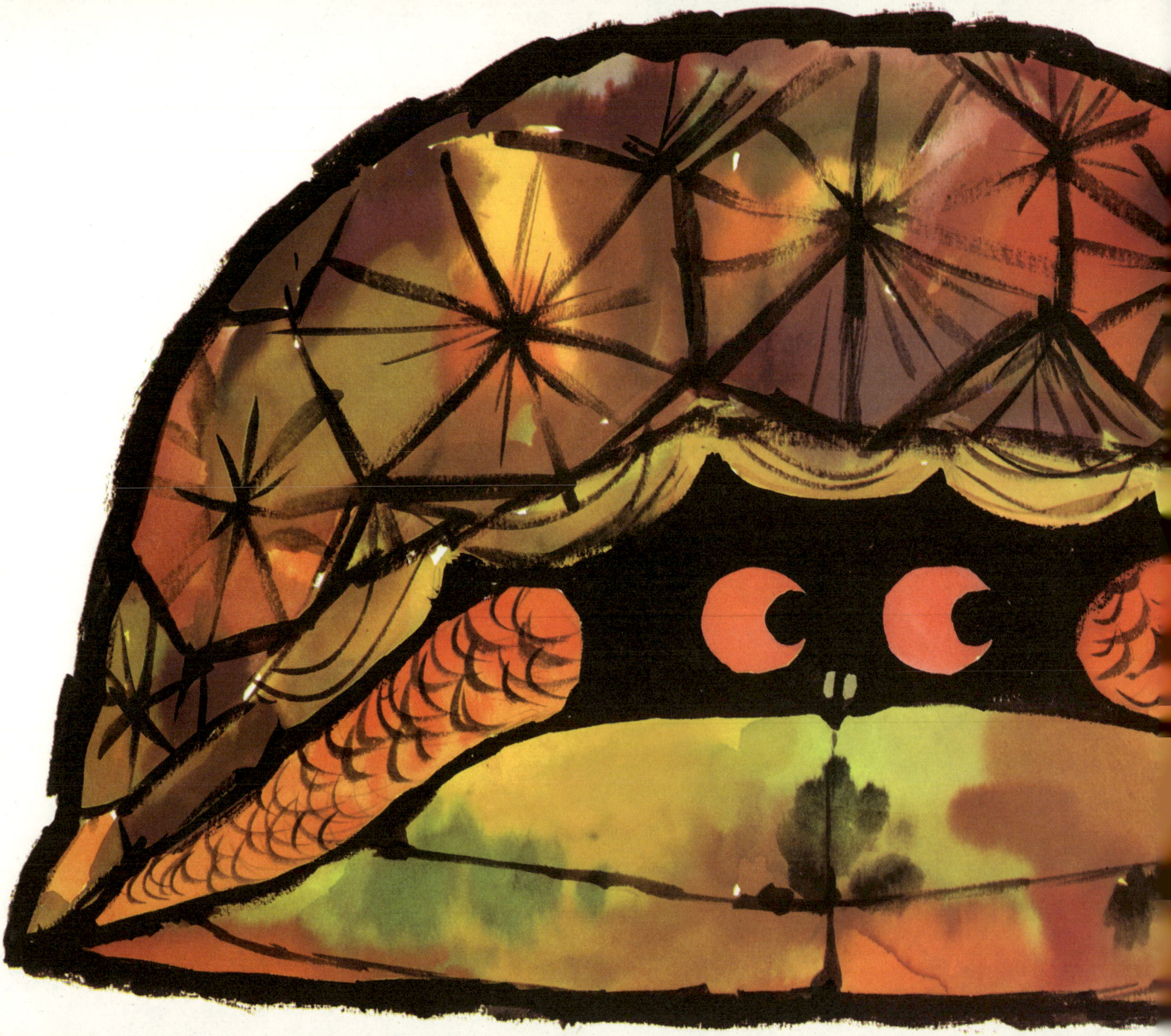

Now here's a shell
with a secret to tell.

Who could dwell
inside this shell?

A mouse in an armor-plated car?
A tiny-toed pigmy dinosaur?

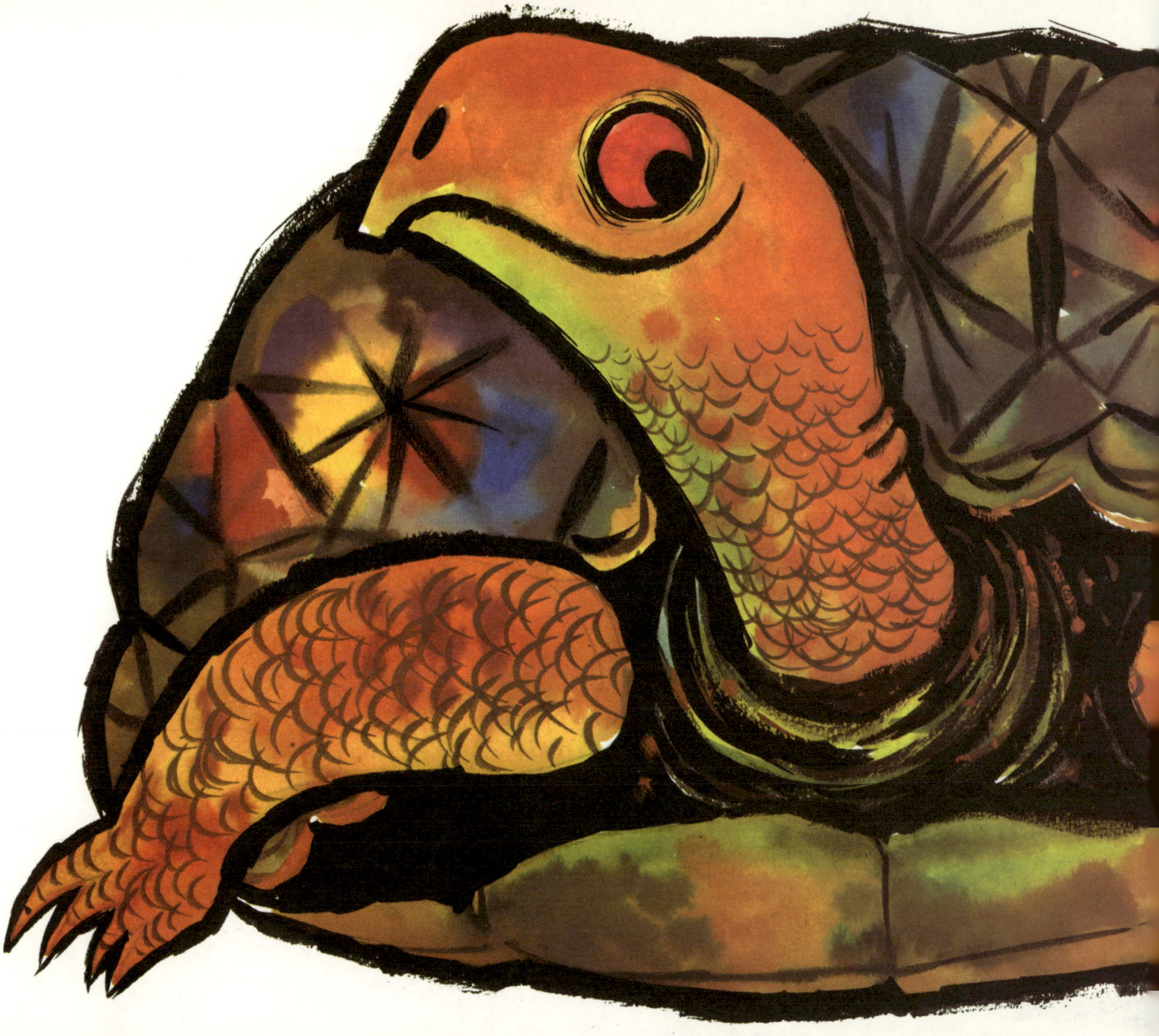

No! Not a dinosaur or mouse,
but a turtle — and the shell's his house.

What's Inside?

Many things dwell
inside a well:
A frog on a log,
a lizard in a hole,
four goldfish and
a small tadpole.
A snapping turtle,
a dragonfly,
and a water bug
who's skittering by.

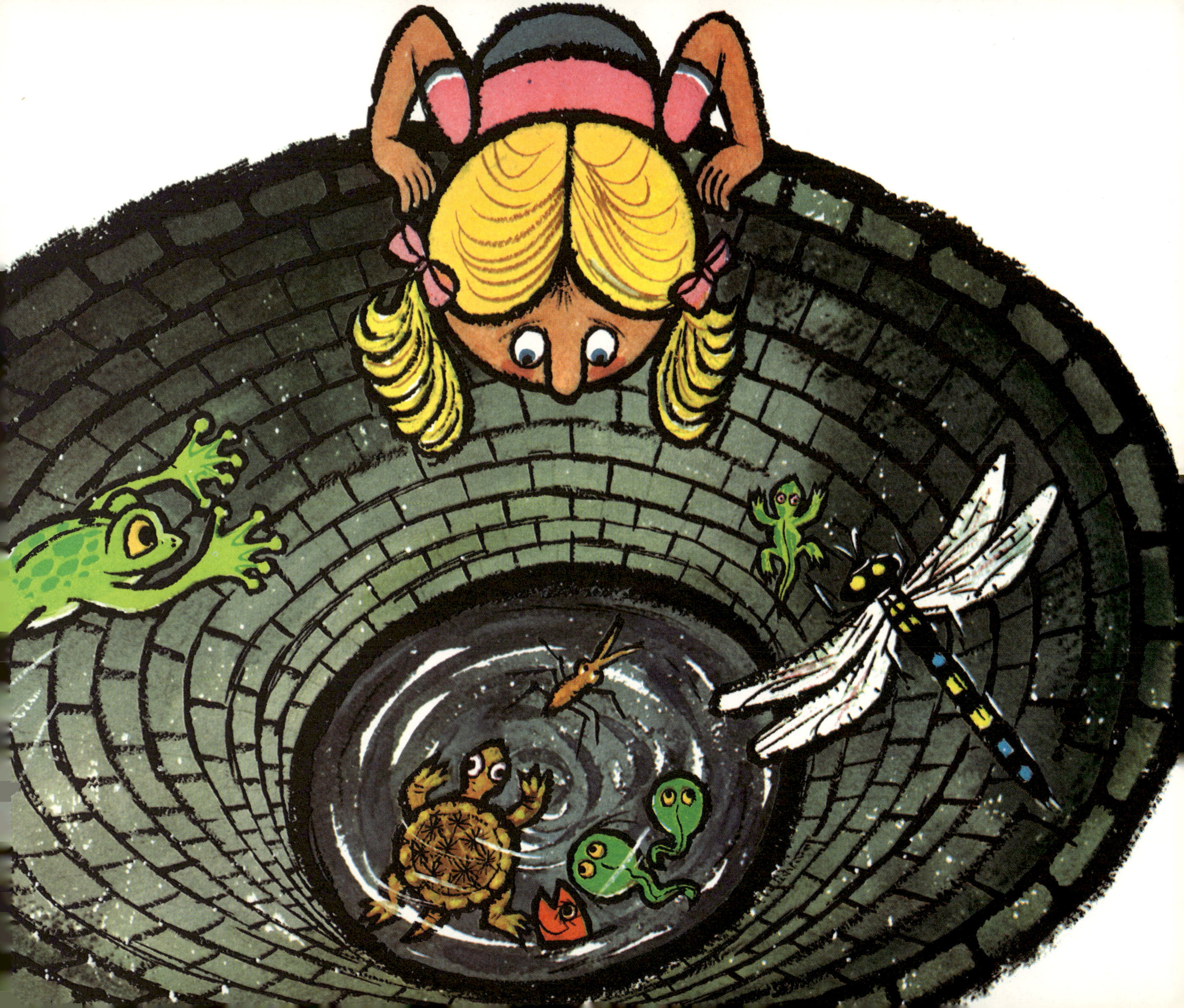

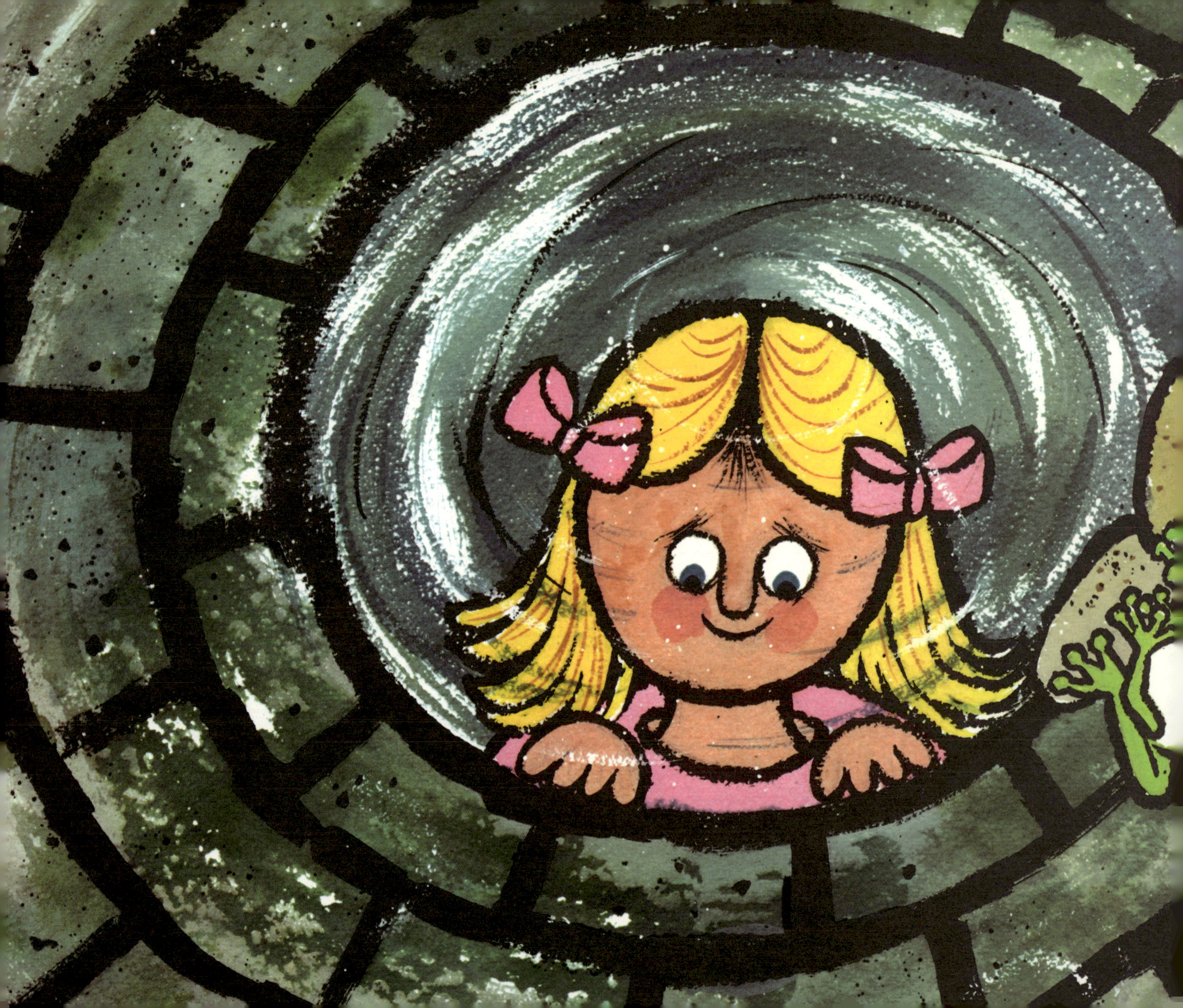

But the most surprising
thing I see
when I look down
is a picture of me!

A silky cocoon
is a small soft room.

Who is there?
A slow-footed slug?
A tired tumblebug?

No! A waking butterfly
about to fly away — goodbye!

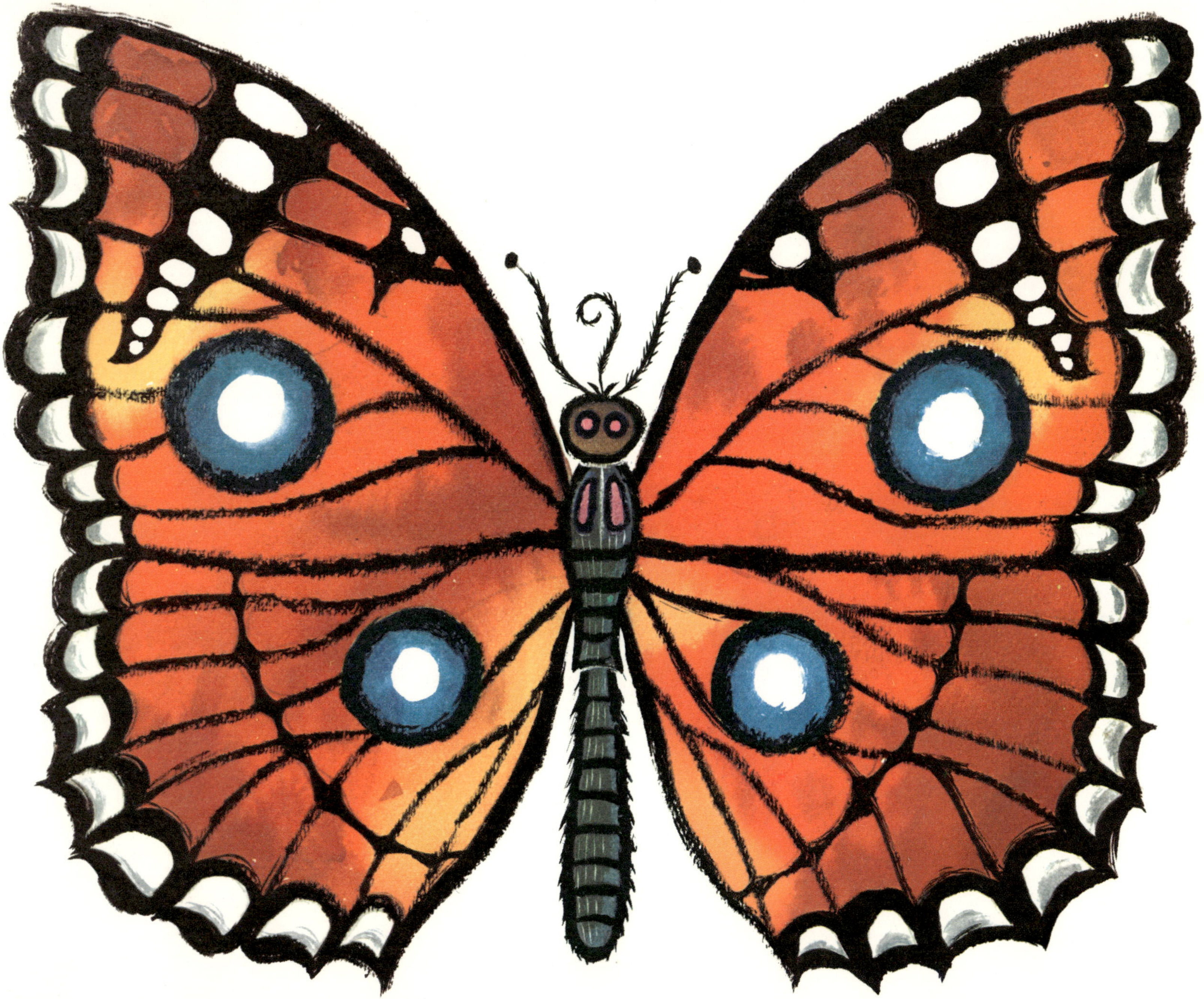